S0-BNH-810

Casting from the Far Bank

By
Fred Laird

Illustrations by Fen Lavanway

PublishAmerica
Baltimore

© 2009 by Fred Laird.
All rights reserved. No part of this book may be reproduced, stored in a retrieval system or transmitted in any form or by any means without the prior written permission of the publishers, except by a reviewer who may quote brief passages in a review to be printed in a newspaper, magazine or journal.

First printing

All characters in this book are fictitious, and any resemblance to real persons, living or dead, is coincidental.

PublishAmerica has allowed this work to remain exactly as the author intended, verbatim, without editorial input.

ISBN: 1-60813-886-0
PUBLISHED BY PUBLISHAMERICA, LLLP
www.publishamerica.com
Baltimore

Printed in the United States of America

Table of Contents

Foreword

When it comes to fishing, there are volumes and volumes of how to books describing everything from knots to casting techniques to different retrieves. All of the information is useful to anyone who wishes to catch fish. There are also numerous books telling of wonderful far off places where one can catch trophy fish in countless numbers. They are well worth reading and dreaming about, though most of us may never venture to them. In this book, I make no attempt to instruct the reader as to how to catch more and better fish, nor do I tease him with accounts of Shangri-Las where he has little hope of treading. This book is not about the science, nor really even the art of fishing. It is about the mystique, the lore, and finally the enjoyment of the sport. While it may not help one catch fish, it is my hope that it will help you enjoy it just a little more when you do (or don't for that matter). May it help to pass a few moments on a day when you are unable to wet a line.

Casting from the Far Bank

The North Shore

They were built during the twenties, thirties, and forties, most of them, the camps on the north shore of the peninsula whose south shore forms Saint Albans Bay on Lake Champlain. The shore itself faces more west than north. I know this from the many evenings that I've stood upon that shore and watched the waning sun draw a gold and crimson path from Wood's Island to my feet. But, the inhabitants of the shore, at least those I know, call it the North Shore and so will I.

Back when the camps were being built, when they cleared the land, they would bulldoze the large boulders that lined the shore to one property line or the other and extend them as far out into the lake as the water level would allow, creating little jetties between the camps. These jetties, in addition to holding fish when the water is high enough, provide an inviting location from which to cast to deeper water. The fact that the buildings were constructed as "camps" rather than the more genteel summer houses and lakefront cottages that line the bay shore is a significant part of their attraction. The North Shore is rocky, rugged, and windswept, and the camps acknowledge the ruggedness and seem less an intrusion of man than would a finely finished house. I feel certain that those who built them realized this. Over the years, the kerosene lanterns and hurricane lamps have given way to electric lights and with electricity, indoor plumbing has become the norm. The water is now pumped up from the lake, rather than carried in buckets. But even today, the smooth paved road that runs along the bay shore becomes a pothole pocked dirt road when you turn to go to the North Shore and the camps still recall the wilder days of yore.

I found myself, one early September afternoon, at the very end of one of the two jetties that define the boundaries of my cousin Ron's camp. The wind was out of the north and it was howling. The waves it created had the rocks awash and my purchase upon them was less than I would have liked. The spray ran off my hat and raingear as though I were standing in a down pour, though it was impossible to discern rain from wind-blown spray. The wind was buffeting me from the right and, of course, I cast right handed thus I had to worry, well not worry, but think about hooking myself with every cast. I had my nine foot, eight weight in hand. More rod than I would have liked, but, I figured, the only thing I had that stood a chance of throwing a fly given the circumstances. I had a size six Mickey Finn on and the big rod did a credible job of getting the smallish streamer out to where the fish might be cruising. Why was I out there? I'd been in the cozy camp, warmed by the kerosene heater, reading an old paperback mystery, happy as a clam when the voice said "lake's beautiful when the nor' wind howls." I hear voices often. Not really hear, but sense, feel, perceive their existence, but I'd not "heard" this one before. I looked out across the lake and admired the beauty and strength of the gale, as it pushed the white caps southward. "Yep" I silently agreed.

"Bet there's some lunkers cruisin' just outside the shore wash." He said. My gaze started to linger longer and longer I felt an urge to grab a rod. I resisted at first. The day wasn't at all inviting. I read a little more. Then he said "ya don't get so many days in which to fish that ya should squander one such as this." The old heavy Vermont accent was palpable.

"But it's a nasty day" I argued.

"And for what did ya spend the money on that fancy rain slicka ya got?" He had a point. I could no longer resist the compulsion. I put the book down, got up, went to the bedroom, drew the curtain that served as a door between it and the living room and changed into clothes appropriate for the occasion. The others in the camp didn't say anything. Ron got that half grin, half grimace that he'd sometimes get when he wanted to call me a fool, but knew it wouldn't do any good. Ron was a fishing fool in his own right and as good a fishing buddy as ever lived. I'm sure, had I asked, he would have ventured out with me, but this particular lunacy I decided to keep for myself. Aunt Bern was deep into her Louis Lamour western and didn't even look up. My wife, Sharon, had grown accustomed to my mild insanity and so said nothing, just looked at me and smiled. If you're ever looking for the definition of true love, there it is. Out the door I went and into the pump house where the rods were stored. I was eyeing my four weight when he said "Better take the big rod and tie on somthin' pretty bright, the water's roiled." I rigged up in the pump house and took a single extra fly with me. I had no intention of opening a fly box while standing on a wet, slippery rock with water on three sides and the wind strong enough to throw me off balance if I weren't careful. One last look at the nice warm camp and I made my way to the end of the jetty. Maybe it was my imagination, but as I reached the half way point, it seemed that the wind, having noticed my presence, picked up ever so slightly. The waves breaking against the rocks sounded almost like laughter, not humorous, but a mean, mocking laughter you might hear from a bully. Maybe it was just Mother Nature trying to scare some sense into me. Maybe it was the lake scoffing at the puny human who dared forth on such a day. "Go on" he said "ya'r just 'bout there anyhow." so I picked my way across the rocks. I found a position where my footing seemed adequate, loosed the fly from the keeper, stripped some line off the reel and made my first cast. It wasn't much of a cast, the wind was having its way with any slack line dangling from the rod or reel, but by holding my rod tip close to the water and sweeping it back as I stripped line from the reel I was able to get enough line out that my next cast would fall near where I wanted it to be. My second cast was better and I had begun to strip the streamer in when it came to sudden stop. The fish ran swiftly for a few minutes, but soon the strength of the rod tired it and I brought it in. It wasn't the largest yellow perch that I'd **ever seen**, but it ranked in the top five and it was the first that I'd **ever** caught on a fly. I'm not inclined to keep most of the fish I catch, but yellow perch are the exception. In my mind, their firm white flesh is second to none on the table and they are prolific to the point that I can't believe that a reasonable harvest can hurt them. I hadn't ventured out that day with yellow perch in mind. Some might say that I hadn't anything in mind, or any mind at all for that matter. Expecting to release whatever I caught, I hadn't taken a stringer with me. I turned and looked back at the pump house. The hundred feet or so looked like a very long way to climb over slippery rocks while carrying a slippery, flopping fish, not to mention the return trip once I had it on the stringer.

The laughter of the waves on the rocks seemed a little louder than before. Suddenly or maybe finally is a better term, an idea came to mind. I knelt carefully, and untied my left boot and removed the lacing. I ran the end through the perch's gill and tied a loop. I then ran the other end through the bottom eye on my boot and tied a quick half hitch. I went back to casting. A few casts later, I had another nice perch on. We call them yellow bellies for the obvious reason, while the bellies of smaller, less mature perch are white. I stood on that jetty for forty five minutes, maybe an hour. I brought in six of the largest perch I'd ever caught. I caught them all on a Mickey Finn. Getting back to land with rod in one hand, stringer in the other, and one loose boot was interesting, but, thankfully, not calamitous. Why was I out there? Who is this he I keep referring to? I'd like to think that maybe the guy who built this camp, half a century or more ago, when it would have been lit by kerosene and heated by wood. Maybe the rugged old man who chose the rugged North Shore for his camp site, maybe he knew from experience that there would be big yellow perch cruising the shore in that kind of weather. Maybe he, looked kindly upon my minor insanity, or saw in me a kindred spirit and decided to reward me with a once in a lifetime experience. Maybe it was he who whispered in my ear to use my bootlace. I feel honored that I was the one he chose to speak to that day. We four sat at the table that evening. The six large perch, home fries, cornbread and spinach made a hell of a meal and the wind blew on.

The next morning the lake was like glass. As the Sun began to cast a path towards Woods Island, I grabbed my four weight rod and made my way to the end of the jetty. I first cast north, where the weeds try to intrude into the calm water between two jetties. After a few casts, failing to get any takes, I turned and faced west toward deeper water. Not too far off in the distance, I could see an old man pulling at the oars of an old Adirondack boat. The sleek double prow craft slid through the water with nary a ripple. Funny, I thought to myself, that I hadn't noticed him, as I walked out onto the jetty. He had a pipe in his mouth and as he leaned into the oars, I could see a little puff of smoke. He stopped rowing for minute, waved then pointed south. I looked to my left in time to spot a swirl from a feeding fish. I took one false cast then landed the fly in the middle of the swirl. Seconds later, I had a tight line on what proved to be about a two pound smallmouth. I turned back toward the old man to thank him for spotting the fish for me. He and his Adirondack had vanished.

Mystic Places

Have you ever been fishing a pool or a riffle or, for that matter, casting along a fog enshrouded lake shore, when you just had to stop fishing for a few moments and take it all in? I certainly hope so. What's more, I suspect so. For, if fishing is enough of your life that you read about it, there's a good chance that the phenomenon has happened to you. At the level of consciousness, you're admiring the beauty of the place, but, at a deeper level, you know that you could do that between casts. It doesn't require that you stop fishing. Besides, it's unlikely that the spot is new to you, you've probably been there before and there is probably nothing more remarkable in its beauty than that of the pool or cove you just left. The fish can be hitting as though they hadn't eaten in a month, or the action can be so slow, you wonder if there are any fish in the water. It doesn't matter. Sometimes you just have to stop, look around, breath deeply, and perhaps sigh before you resume casting. It may just be that you're being spoken to. No, you don't hear anything, except the breeze in the trees, or the gurgling of the stream, but that may be because the message is ever so slightly beyond your audible range, subliminal if you will, in the myriad of sounds around you.

It happens to me frequently, more frequently on moving water than on still, but it does happen on still water as well. At first, I thought I was just admiring nature but, overtime, I've come to realize that, in these moments, I'm absorbing nature and somehow being absorbed by it. Maybe the ghost of some old fisherman is coaching me, or simply wishing me success for the day. It might be the spirit of one of our nation's early inhabitants, wondering at the complexity of the equipment I'm using. Perhaps it's the soul of some great lunker fish that swam these waters in bygone days, chiding me to respect its descendents.

Some think I've gone loony when I talk about such things. I guess it hasn't happened to them…yet. And those of us who are fortunate enough to have it happen know that it certainly is not lunacy, but most probably some of our sanest moments. All I know is that it comes upon me more often when I'm alone than with somebody, but it does sometimes happen when I'm fishing with someone who's a true fisherman, or someone who is especially close to me. It never happens to me on "busy water", amid throngs of fishermen or a lot of boat traffic. Maybe I'm just less receptive under those conditions, or maybe the spirits shy away from crowds and clamor. It happens to me more often in the early morning, or near dusk, but has happened in midday, when the sunlight was glistening off the water in an almost hypnotic fashion. It's a wonderful sense of peace, of belonging, of being a part of a brotherhood of fishers whose beginning is ancient beyond written history. It so enhances the act of fishing that if it were to stop happening to me, I might hang up my rods. Why it happens where it happens, I don't pretend to know, but I am ever so thankful for the "mystic places" and the spirits that inhabit them.

Out Early

You're walking down the path to the dock, nothing stirs. The gray fog lying on the water is a slightly different shade than that of the rest of your immediate world. All is silent and chill and damp. Dew hangs from a spider's web alongside the path you travel. As you near the lake's edge, you can see that the fog is a foot or so deep, not really hiding the water, but turning the surface into a dark, opaque, sheet. You get to the boat, loose the lines, and ease it out of its slip. A moment ago, you thought you were alone, but now the dervishes and ballerinas that dwell in the morning mist start to dance and swirl in front of and behind the boat. You sit there, take a sip from the thermos of coffee, dark, rich, hot, that you brought along, and watch as they point this way and that, as though directing where you should make your first cast of the day. You take another sip. You almost hate to crank the motor. It's as though mechanical technology doesn't quite belong in the moment. But, crank it you do, and the fog bound denizens react accordingly, furiously spinning and flowing to escape the path of the boat, and some to follow along behind it. The voices that have been talking to you, the ones you don't really hear, having won the debate with the others that would have sent you to the dam at the east end, or the cliffs to the north, have convinced you to start fishing at the finger at the west end of the lake, where the feeder creek deposits its flotsam and nutrients into the lake, so you head west. As you do, the first rays of the sun fall on your back then light a path on the lake in front of you. This awakens the rest of the dwellers of the mist and they begin to flee into the still dark woods where the land meets the water. You notice a doe and two fawns drinking from one of the coves to which the mist has fled. You cut the motor, drop the electric, and grab your six weight. It is almost time for the first cast of the day, but you hesitate, another sip of coffee. As with all things exquisite, better to prolong the moment than to act in haste.

Ron's Lucky Hat

We all know, we fishermen that is, that luck plays a major part in the pastime that we pursue. We all have some kind of good luck charm that we carry with us whenever we set out to battle the various creatures that live on the other side of the surface. I'm not talking about the one week a year guy, or the guy who "likes to fish, but never finds the time", I'm talking about those of us who were born to fish, who can't imagine not fishing, those of us to whom fishing is a passion. It's as though we believe that without some lucky edge, we have little chance of prevailing against the myriad forces that stand between us and our prey. While some of us have rituals that we perform and others eat "lucky meals" before a trip, in my experience, the most common "good luck charm" is the lucky hat. Few of us, however, are able to explain why that particular chapeau brings us luck.

My cousin Ron, one of my very favorite fishing partners until he passed away last year, had a lucky hat. One night, a few years ago, while when the rods were in and the suds were out, I asked him just what made it "a lucky hat". He replied that, though it had been some years (and the hat looked it) he recalled, vividly, the first time that he had worn it and how he had landed several nice pike and smallmouth that day.

"Okay, Ron," I said "that's how you came to know that it was lucky, but how'd you come by it and why'd you wear it the first time? Didn't you already have a "lucky hat"? What happened to that and why weren't you wearing it?" Ron could see that this was going to be another of our deep philosophical conversations, so he twisted another cap and shifted around on one of the old sofas that furnished the camp overlooking Lake Champlain, not far from St. Albans Bay, Vermont. It was dark out now, and the wind was down so that the lake played a haunting tune as it lapped gently upon the gray slate shore. Off in the distance, the lights of the toll bridge at Rousses Point winked at us, as though they knew something was adrift. It seemed just the right backdrop to explore this concept of "luck".

"I was down to Getchel's Store to get some steaks and burgers for a weekend on the lake, they always have the best beef." Ron started. "That's when I saw the hat on a rack by the front door. Hell I don't know what it was about that particular hat, it wasn't much different than the dozen or so others that were hanging with it, but I liked it, so I picked it up." Ron took a sip of his beer and I took the opportunity to interrupt.

"See that's what I'm getting at. You don't know why you decided to buy the hat. I can tell you and it's like I've been telling you for a while now. They were talking to you. No, you didn't hear anything, but there was something in the breeze, or the angle of the sun, the way the birds were singing, something. They were telling you that the magic in your old hat was just about used up and it was time to get a new one. They picked it out for you. They put you in the store when that hat was visible on the rack. They didn't let some one else get it first. Your fishing spirits were looking out for you on that day. A day you weren't even fishing. Ron, I think that makes you a little special in their eyes and that's a lot better than lucky."

Ron looked at me with that look that he could get, kind of half grin half grimace, that said "Oh no here we go again!"

I was undaunted. "So now you've told me how you bought it, but you haven't explained why you were wearing it instead of your former lucky hat."

"Damnedest thing" he said. "We got to camp late Friday night, unloaded the car and settled in so that we could get an early start on the Lake in the morning. I was the first one up. I put the coffee on and went out to the shed to get my gear around. I reached for my hat, on the nail, just inside the door, right above the fishing rods. You know where I keep it. It wasn't there. I was sure I'd hung it up there last weekend, before I left, but it wasn't there. I looked on the floor and all around the shed, but there was no sign of it. Well, I got a couple of rods rigged up and headed back to the camp for a cup of mud before heading out. That's when I saw the raccoon tracks outside the shed. I figure one of those rascally critters must have found his way into the shed, it isn't exactly air tight you know, and made off with my hat. Only thing I could think of. So I grabbed something to eat, put on my new hat, for lack of any other, and headed out. And what a day it turned out to be. I motored up into Lapan's Bay and trolled around for an hour or so. Brought in three healthy pike, kept the smallest for supper and released the others. Then I went over to the near side of Wood's Island, where I picked up several nice smallmouth, two and a half to three and a half pounders. On the way back to camp, I stopped at the edge of the weed bed out front and got a dozen nice yellow belly perch to go with the pike. It wasn't even noon, and I was fished out. So it became my lucky hat."

"So you think it was all just happenstance huh." I chimed in. "You really think a raccoon made off with your hat? Doesn't sound any more plausible to me than the spirits took it away! But even if you're right, even if some four legged, masked bandit absconded with your hat, what made the varmint do it and why just then? That shed's been full of holes for years, why'd it happen that week? See what I mean? You were guided to that hat and practically forced to wear it. The magic that it holds for you comes from a place well beyond the hat itself."

Ron shook his head a little, or maybe it was a nod. He gazed out the window at the pathway to the sky that Champlain beguiles us with on certain clear nights, when the moon is running near to full. Then he turned and said. "Yeah, Fred, I guess you're right, but enough of this deep thinking stuff. Let's play some cribbage!"

The First Time

The day was warm enough to be late spring, but spring was still a week or more away. This was our first time together. Oh, I'd held her before and admired her beauty. She was long and slender, sort of honey blonde, maybe a little darker, but this was the first time we were actually going to do something. I had been planning it since we fist met, about four months earlier. We were going off by ourselves this weekend, away from prying eyes, inquisitive noses, and the world in general. I'd been dreaming of it all week, losing concentration at work during the day as I anticipated the moment. She was older than I, though I didn't know how much. It didn't matter, she was lovely and I wanted to be with her.

It didn't start off that well. At first our movements were clumsy, awkward, and ineffective. She seemed slow to respond, or perhaps, I was trying to rush things. I held her too roughly, or not tightly enough. She felt rigid and unwilling to flex, but we kept trying, and before too long, we started to get our rhythm. Our movements began to compliment one another. I flexed my muscle and she bent gracefully to the force, then she sprang back, showing her own strength. We moved as one, back and forth, arching, straightening, and then bending again. For forty five minutes we continued the dance, pausing only briefly, now and then to change positions. I knew then that she was truly mine. That we would share many such times in the coming summer months. There would be others of course. She was too old and fragile to be the only one. For the moment, however, she was my queen. When the day was over, I broke her down. I carefully handled each of her three sections, gently placing them back in the tube, careful not to drop them to the bottom, or jamb any guides. After all, a good bamboo fly rod is hard to come by these days.

The Summer of the Boat

The morning sun was cresting the ridge on the east side of the North Branch River and beginning to light the top of Wrightsville Dam. The subtle change in air temperature that it caused began to lift the morning mist that until now had all but obscured the two young boys scaling the scree on their way to the top. The two lads, we'll call them Charlie and Fred since those were their names, actually, Charlie's name was David, but we called him Charlie then, so we'll call him Charlie now. As for Fred, well my name was always Fred and though I've been called other things, I see no need to mention them here. As I was saying, they were toting their fishing rods, two cans of night crawlers they'd caught the night before, a genuine war surplus canteen filled with water, and a couple of peanut butter and jelly sandwiches, which meant they were good for the day. It was mid to late July and this was the fifth or sixth time the two had climbed the dam since school had let out in June, but this trip was to prove different than the previous ones. As was their habit, they paused at the top to try to throw a few rocks into the reservoir. Fred, being a year older and larger than Charlie had the advantage, but Charlie held his own. The two then continued down the wet side of the dam to the east corner where the spillway was located. They always started fishing there in the back water that the spillway created and it was one of the better spots they had found. Today though, the spillway yielded nothing, so they worked their way around the east shore, stopping wherever the brush would allow them to make a cast. They weren't having much luck, so they pushed on, exploring further around the lake than they had ever gone before. They came upon a decent sized cove where they discovered an old wooden boat pulled up on shore and tied off to one of the saplings that pretty much concealed it from sight. They had no idea to whom the boat belonged, nor did they know how long it had been there. They assumed that someone had brought it down the old dirt road that lead from the state highway to the far side of the impoundment and had decided to leave it, rather than load it in and out every time they wanted to use it. No, they didn't know who the owner was, but for today, the boat was theirs. There were no oars with the boat so they whittled away at a couple of the saplings with their pocket knives and soon had two poles with which to propel their newfound craft. They polled out into the middle of the cove and dropped their lines, feeling pretty good about being able to fish from a boat. The boat took on a little water but nothing that a bit of bailing now and then couldn't keep up with. Later, as they gained confidence, they ventured out into the main lake area, being careful to stay near enough to shore to maintain poling depth. That evening, the sandwiches gone, the canteen near empty and a nice stringer of perch hanging from the side of the boat, they returned it to the place where they had found it, leaving it as precisely as they had found it as they could and traipsed toward the dam on the other side of which was Charlie's home. They were excited about the boat and talked over one another about all the things they would do that summer, now that they were no longer land bound. When they reached the top of the dam, they stopped to catch their breath and renew their rock throwing. And there they made a solemn pledge, as young boys will do, to never tell anyone about the boat. They knew in their hearts that if their mothers were aware that they were afloat in the reservoir that they would be banned from ever going there again, much less using the boat. After all, it had only been three years since old Caleb Fletcher had drowned up there. He'd been Charlie's nearest neighbor until then. His wife had passed years before and he lived alone in a tiny cottage just down the road from Charlie's house. The story was he had fallen out of his old rowboat and either hit his head, or was too old to make it to shore. They had to drag the reservoir for a couple of days before they recovered his body. His boat had been found washed up on the east shore, blown there by the wind. Nobody ever went to the trouble of removing it. It was just left there to rot. But that was three years ago the boys had been just six and seven respectively and they knew none of this first hand, only what they'd been told. He'd been a good soul, nice to the boys, always puffing on his corncob pipe, the scent of Prince Albert in the summer evening air, as they sat on his front porch and he regaled them with fishing yarns. The boys would take him cookies, or a piece of pie or cake whenever they visited him. Charlie's mom, Bern, had told the boys that Caleb had cancer, a death sentence back in those days. One evening, when the boys asked him about it, he told them that it made no never mind that he'd die fishing like it was meant to be. As the young and innocent will do, they just accepted what he said.

The boys were pretty sure if some of the older boys caught wind of the boat their own usage would be at peril, so they made a blood oath not to tell. Down the dry side they went, talking and dreaming of adventures to come in their boat. They quieted down as they neared Charlie's house, lest someone hear them. The perch were cleaned and put in the refrigerator for tomorrow's meal. Tonight was red flannel hash night. Bern made the best red flannel hash in the world, at least in my world, and, no matter how big my world became, my opinion never changed. There were glances and smirks between the two boys at the dinner table, and the grown-ups could sense something was amiss, but they didn't know what.

The next morning the boys were up and out early. Fred had spent the night at Charlie's house and they had slipped out before any of the grownups had awakened. They had their canteen, but today's lunch was crackers and cheese. Too much noise and time involved in making pbj sandwiches. This morning, their rock throwing was cut short, so anxious were they to return to the boat. Down the wet side they scrambled. No stopping at the spillway or any of their other usual spots. Today they would spend the whole day afloat. The boat was there. Their poles were still in it, and there were no footprints in the mud, save their own from yesterday. They had even brought along an extra can for bailing. Yesterday, they had had to consolidate their night crawlers into one can, but today they each had their own. The fishing was great, a lot of perch, a couple of pickerel, a couple of bull pout. Though they spent the whole day in the boat, it went quickly. They noticed the sun starting to set behind the western ridge and they knew they'd be late for supper. They poled back to where they'd found the boat and, once again, left it just as they had found it. They made their way up and over the dam. No talking this time, saving their breath for the climb and no stopping to throw rocks.

They hit the screen door that opened into Charlie's kitchen about thirty minutes past supper time. They deposited the fish in the kitchen sink, went to the bathroom to wash their hands and sat down silently at the table. No smirks and giggles tonight, they knew they were in trouble. Bern and Jean, Fred's mom and Bern's sister, sat there staring at the two boys, relieved that they were home safe, but angry that they were late. It had been one of the conditions of allowing the two to fish the dam that they would be home by supper every night and this was the first time that the boys had failed to keep their end of the bargain. There were still a few perch on the platter and a couple of baked potatoes and some succotash left so the boys silently loaded their plates and began to eat, eyes down, concentrating mightily on the food, as though that would protect them from their mothers' ire. Just then, the boys' aunt Molly came through the kitchen door, carrying a six pack of Carling Black Label. She plopped it on the table and began telling how she had seen the queerest thing that afternoon as she was driving up state route twelve toward Putnam.

Seems she had glanced down onto the Wrightsville Dam waters and had seen a boat. So she slowed down to take a better look. About now the boys were sure their respective gooses were cooked so they lowered their heads even more. Then Molly swore that it was none other than Caleb Fletcher out in that boat. Now the boys had been there all day and they knew that there was no one else on the water. There had been no other boat that Molly could have mistaken for that of Caleb Fletcher's and they couldn't see how she could have mistaken two young boys for one old man, much less one three years dead, but they said nothing.

The ladies were all three talking now, each with a bottle of Carling in their hand, when Jean thought to question the boys. Had they seen an old man in a boat while they were fishing? The truthful reply was, of course, no. The banter kept on for quite a while, with suggestions that Molly have her eyes, head, or both examined. The boys finished eating, got up and washed their dishes, cleaned the fish they had brought home and slipped out of the house to search for night crawlers. Jean and Fred went back to their place in Montpelier that night so there was no fishing the dam for a while.

Several days later, they were back in Wrightsville. Charlie and Fred, thinking that the last misadventure had been forgotten, were all set to fish the dam. As they rounded up their gear and bait, they heard Bern admonish them not to be late and if they saw some crazy old coot in a boat, to stay clear of him. The boys said they would and headed for the dam. At the top, they carefully surveyed the water. They could see no one upon it. They headed for the boat, not stopping to fish the spillway or any of their other favorite spots. Again they found it much as they had left it, no footprints in the mud around it, but there in the bottom of the boat lay an empty Prince Albert tobacco tin. It looked old, but Charlie pocketed it, figuring it would be good for holding worms. They shoved off and poled out to a point that had produced the pickerel on the last trip. They baited up and began fishing. They were a little worried about being spotted, but guessed that they were too far from the main road for anybody to recognize them. Certainly, Molly hadn't. As they were fishing, a sudden strong gust of wind hit the boat broadside. It carried the boat at least twenty feet further from shore before the boys realized what had happened. They dropped their rods in the bottom of the boat and grabbed their poles, but they had been carried beyond poling depth and the wind was not relenting. They were now at its mercy. Eventually, it deposited them on the far shore from whence they'd started the day. They knew they hadn't enough time to return the boat to its rightful place and still be home by dinner, so they hid it with the branches of some nearby scrub pines and headed for home. They hiked up the old dirt road that lead down from the state highway and then walked the shoulder of route twelve back to the top of the dam. From there, they took their usual route down the dry side. This brought them to the house about an hour before they were due. But, when questioned, they responded that the fishing had been slow so they decided to come home early. That night and into the next morning the wind howled and the rain came down in buckets so there was no thought of going back to the boat. The boys played games and cards and, when they were pretty sure no one could hear them, they wondered in whispers whether the boat would be alright. At least, they reckoned, the rightful owner of the boat wouldn't be about in this weather either. They hardly slept that night. By morning, the rain had stopped and while the predawn sky was gray and full of mist, the boys figured that it would be a good day to fish. With rods, drink and food in hand, they once again headed up the dam. This time, however, once at the top, they turned west toward the service road that led to where they had stashed the boat. When they reached the stand of scrub pines, they were beside themselves. The boat wasn't there. Certainly, they thought, it was too heavy to have been blown away, even by a wind such as last night's. They searched around for a while then figured the owner must have found it and returned it to his original hiding spot. It seemed curious though, that he would have been out on a day such as yesterday. Dismayed, they decided to fish their way around the north end of the reservoir to where the boat would surely be. But, a few hours later, when they reached the cove where it had been tied, all they found was the old rotted carcass of a homemade rowboat that certainly hadn't floated for years and a nearly imperceptible waft of Prince Albert in the air.

The Five Pounder

It was twilight as we launched. Twilight, that magical, mystical, ephemeral period when the stars are visible, but only barely so and all things seem slightly of another world. Some call it dusk, but for me twilight conjures up a lyrical beauty that is more appropriate when speaking of that time of evening as it falls upon a lake. Anyway, supper was in our bellies and Champlain was calm and my cousin, Ron, and I had decided to troll Lapan's Bay before we settled in at the card table for the night. The sun was all but gone behind Wood's Island as we set out. It was not much different than many other evenings when we had done so, perhaps a little later than some, but the Siren song of the water lapping the slate at water's edge seemed a little more alluring than usual. Earlier in the week, we had found that this was a good hour to collect a pike or two and trolling to be the most efficacious method of doing so. We launched the boat and positioned it some forty yards off shore and began putting north. I was dragging a red and white Daredevil and Ron had on a weed-less Johnson's silver minnow with a pork rind. Up into Lapan's Bay we went, entering on the south point and trying to stay right on the edge off the weed beds that we couldn't see but knew were there. By the time we exited the bay, fishless I might add, twilight had turned to dark and if twilight is an exotic and mysterious time, dark is just dark.

"Ron" I said "looks like the fishing gods were just teasing us tonight, do you think its time to head back to camp and play some cribbage?"

"Let's troll our way back, I've just got a feeling" he replied "we'll go down to the south end of Wood's then cut across to camp."

"Suits me" I said and started to say something about Ron's "feeling" but caught myself. I examined the vast night sky. Maybe it was just me, but the twinkling stars seemed to have a mischievous mirth about them. I looked north and could see the lights of the Rousses point draw bridge winking at us, but not necessarily amiably. Ron and I had held many a discussion about such things with my contention being the "feelings" were actually some extra-sensory communications from the fishing spirits and Ron pretty much thinking that I was full of hooey. Now some, many, most of you may side with Ron. It confounds me that you believe in luck (and I never met a fisherman that didn't) but not in unseen forces or spirits. But what transpired next went a long way toward swaying Ron to my way of thinking.

For those unfamiliar with Lake Champlain, let me tell you, it is a large body of water. It is over a hundred miles long, separating Vermont from New York State for most of their common border and extending into Canada at its northern end. It varies in width from less than a mile to several miles and runs from very shallow bays to hundreds of feet deep. The area we were trolling was twenty to thirty feet in depth. It is necessary that you appreciate the volume of the lake to understand that what happened next nears mathematical impossibility.

We were trolling along and had probably made half the length of Wood's Island when Ron's rod bent severely.

"Snag" I cursed as I kicked the motor into neutral. Ron agreed. Remembering that Ron had rigged a weed-less lure, I again cursed his bad luck (or the work of the fishing gods if you see things as I do). Ron commenced to lifting and reeling, hoping to be able to drag the offending object to the boat and recover his spoon. About the third lift, the "snag" seemed to make a short run. Ron let out a whoop and yelled "fish". I hadn't really been paying attention. I was trying to watch the angle of the line as it met the water to see if we were getting over top of the snag, but with his shout I turned to see what he was up to. It looked to me like he was pulling us back to the snag point but, just as I was about to turn away again, it made another short run. I saw it. It wasn't his imagination. We continued for about thirty minutes, gaining line, loosing line but making progress. Finally, Ron began steadily cranking in the line.

"Must have tired him out" he said, though there was still a mighty bend in his rod.

Then I caught a glimpse of his lure, but saw no fish. I turned to Ron to commiserate his bad luck of loosing the fish after such a struggle but saw that his rod was still bent. I grabbed the line and hand hauled the remaining few feet into the boat and there, impaled neatly on the single, weed guarded hook was a piece of braided polypropylene rope. Twenty five or so feet later, I hauled up a five pound bell anchor. We sat there stunned. Somebody had cut his anchor line, probably had backed over it. We guessed that the "runs" were the anchor falling off ledges as Ron dragged it toward the boat. We fished no more that night. We beat a hasty retreat to the camp, the man in the moon grinning at our backs as we did. So all you nay sayers out there, you calculate the odds of snagging a half inch diameter rope with a single, weed guarded hook in a body of water the size of Champlain. Then you tell me that there are no forces at work influencing the success of our fishing adventures.

The Morning Feed

It was not unlike any other work day morning. I had arrived early and had spread out the drawings on the kitchen counter of the high end condo unit that we were building out for the purchaser. It was about ten to seven, when the little unheard voices that sometimes whisper to my subconscious mind began to speak to me. They were coaxing me, urging me to go to the living room window that overlooks the Potomac River, just down stream from Key Bridge, and directly onto Roosevelt Island. It was almost starting time and I considered ignoring them, but, in the end, I decided follow their suggestion. I find that I always do as the voices direct me. Otherwise, I probably wouldn't know they were there. I don't really hear them, but when I find myself doing something for no apparent reason or deciding upon one thing rather than another, without knowing why, I figure it's the voices. I don't know, with certainty, to whom the voices belong. I figure they are the spirits of bygone souls who recognize in me the love they held for fishing and all things that are part of the pursuit of the sport/art. Whoever they are, they seldom steer me wrong. From the angle of the window, I could see half of the island, from the upstream end to a point of rocks that juts out into the main body of the river. The sun was rising and had begun to glisten off the small ripples made by the gentle morning breeze. At first, that was all I saw, but the voices urged me to look more closely. Then I glimpsed a silver flash, near the point of rocks, then another, a little upstream, then another and another. I stood entranced, staring out the window, guessing that I was watching a school of white perch feeding on some smaller forage fish. I noticed, too, that there were dimples on the surface, growing in increasing numbers. Either the baitfish were being chased to the surface, or some insect hatch was occurring simultaneously with the feeding frenzy below and was becoming a part of it. Then a huge splash caught my eye, then a second and a third and more. Large fish, probably school sized striped bass, had joined the carnage, no doubt feeding on the perch as they pursued the smaller fish. It was magnificent to watch. I could almost hear Tchaikovsky as the ballet progressed, swirls and flashes, dimples and splashes, moving up and down the island shore. It lasted about twenty minutes, making me late getting the job started, but there was no way I was able to tear myself away from the spectacle. I wasn't fishing that day, but the fishing gods, those minor deities that send me to one cove, rather than another, or compel me to fish one stretch of river, rather than the one above or below it, had invited me to be part of the Morning Feed. I could envision myself standing on that rock point, rod in hand. Had I been, I suspect I would have been too taken by the moment to have made a cast.

The Bamboo Rod

They were talking to me again. The fishing gods had been whispering in my ear for about a year and a half, maybe two years now. I started yearning for a bamboo fly rod about then. There was no particular reason, no memorable event to cause the yen, but there it was working on me, eating away at my resistance. I recall my father fishing with one, even trying to teach me to cast with it, but I don't remember that it held any significance for me at the time. I know not the fate of the rod that he used, probably lost or damaged in one of the many moves of my childhood. Never the less, I began obsessing for a bamboo fly rod. Now I'm no snob when it comes to tackle. Matter of fact, I would probably be considered on the cheap side. I want utilitarian equipment. I don't want trash that isn't going to function when called upon, but I don't want to be carrying something that will affect my decision, whether to jump to the next rock or not. I want to own my gear, not have it own me. All that said, in spite of the fact that I have at least one fly rod for every situation that I can imagine myself in, I simply had to have a bamboo rod. Not something new, you understand, something from days of yore, when bamboo was king of the rivers, something that had a story behind it, a history. A rod that had landed lunkers back in the days of gut leaders and silk lines, that's what I wanted. The only reason I can think of that I would want such a relic is that those pesky minor deities that control the wonderful world of piscatorial adventure were telling me to fish with one. I looked at many in various antique shops and the like, but didn't find any that "felt" right. I admired some that were owned by others, but not for sale. I heard of a few for sale that were gone by the time I got there. I searched classified ads and local trading pamphlets, but nothing really caught my eye. Then, one day, a coworker introduced me to E-Bay. Initially, I was in heaven. There were literally hundreds to choose from at any given time! My problem became a new one. There were literally hundreds to choose from at any given time! Days turned into weeks and then months as I perused the listings. I saw many that were, or at least sounded, beautiful, but were much too dear for my wallet. I saw a few that I thought I'd like to own, but somehow I was always outbid. I began to dislike the other people on E-bay until it dawned on me (probably due to an inaudible whispering in my ear) that my competition was probably experiencing the same inexplicable desire to own an old bamboo rod that I was. They were kindred spirits. Why else would they be bidding on a bamboo fly rod. The fishing gods were talking to them, just as they were to me. The rods that they were winning were the rods the gods wanted them to have. When the rod I was meant to use came along, I'd somehow end up with it.

Then it happened. It was advertised as a Flash. From the research I'd done, I figured that meant it was a Montague. Not a special rod, to be sure, but a serviceable one. It was said to be in good, useable condition. I stayed on the computer right down to the wire and then made my final bid. A few minutes later, I was informed that the rod was mine. It wasn't long, though it seemed that it was, until the rod arrived. When I removed it from its tube, I saw that one snake guide needed to be rewound. I was kind of glad. It was as though the gods were forcing me to personalize it, make it mine, or maybe they were making me belong to it. It's an eight and a half footer. I'm sensing it will handle a six weight line. There is nothing to tell me this. It's just the way it "feels". Or, maybe somebody whispered the fact in my ear, but I didn't quite hear the words. Funny how that possibility always seems to be there.

Anyway, we're near the end of February as I write this. Another month and the sunnies will be stirring in the nearby pond. That is where Flash and I will first become one, where I will learn how to handle the slow, full length curve of bamboo, as opposed to the fast, power butt, whip tip action of graphite. A lesson that suddenly seems long over due. A small sunfish pond may be a rather mundane beginning for what I suspect will be a long and wonderful companionship, but most good things are better taken slowly. As we come to know one another, as Flash learns to bend gracefully at the end of my arm, and land the fly where it should land, I am certain the gods will find wonderful places for us to go and great fish for us to meet. Thus the lore and history of Flash will grow and, in time, a decade or two, I will pass it all on. The gods will whisper in some one's ear and they will begin to yearn for a bamboo relic of another time. I have a one year old grandson now. If the gods are just and kind, as I believe them to be, I have a pretty good idea of who that some one will be.

Humility

If I needed a reminder that the fishing gods have a sense of humor, I certainly got one during my recent trip to Florida. For months, they had been whispering in my ear that it was time for me to try my hand at fly casting in the surf. They had painted visions of a glass smooth ocean stretched out benignly before me while a bright orange ball emerged from the other side of the world. I was knee deep in the water, casting to the denizens that cruised up and down the beach seeking smaller fish as prey. They had told me that my nine weight travel rod would be sufficient for the purpose and that I would surely be rewarded with at least one admirable fish.

It was the week after Thanksgiving. Sharon, my wife, and I were staying in Cocoa Beach. The excuse for the trip was to do some work on a condo that we own in Mims, but I was determined to find some time to fish, particularly to fly cast into the surf. I awoke Monday morning and stepped out the door. The wind nearly took it from my hand. I ducked back inside and turned on The Weather Channel. When the local weather came on, I was informed that the wind was out of the east at fifteen to twenty, with gusts to thirty. I decided that my excursion to the deep blue could wait another day. Tuesday proved to be no better, so we had a leisurely breakfast at the Sunrise Diner which we had discovered the day before and renewed our efforts to improve the condo. We did find some time to fish from the pier at Jetty Park, with some success too. Wednesday morning was more of the same, but by now I was beginning to panic. How dare the fishing gods fill my mind with such visions and then throw near gale force winds in my face! So! I put on my gear, told Sharon I'd be back in an hour or two, and headed for the beach. It was a short drive to the spot I'd chosen to try my venture and, as I parked my truck in the lee of the dunes, it seemed as though I might prevail after all. I'm sure that by now the god, or gods that had been responsible for initiating my folly, had called many of their friends around whatever device they use to observe us mortals, and that the Asgard of the fishing gods was echoing with laughter and jocularity at my expense. I climbed the wooden walkway that lead over the dune and the wind it me full in the face. I could almost see them elbowing one another and pointing at me. Undaunted, I traversed the beach, waded about knee deep into the surf, loosed the deceiver from the hook keeper and began to play out line, thinking somehow that I'd be able to cast into the gale. I was, of course, mistaken. If I timed it just right, I could throw about twenty five or so feet, but the first wave to find my fly would pick it up and deposit at my feet, or behind me, or somewhere else equally annoying. The out-rushing water swept the sand from beneath my feet and I found it increasingly difficult to maintain an upright position. Then, a late breaking wave hit me just below the belt. It took the last of my determination and swept it out to sea. I know the gods were having trouble maintaining their equilibrium, so hard their laughter must have been. Defeated, I made my retreat to my truck and stowed my rod and gear. As I drove back the room, I thought about what had just taken place. Obviously, the fishing gods had decided that I needed a comeuppance. I'm not sure why, but then I'd be the last to recognize the reason, though I will ponder it a while. And I still have my dream of facing the calm Atlantic sunrise to experience over and over again until it's fulfilled.

The Lesson

It came over me as though I were twelve again, a sense of urgent excitement, as I fondled my new Cahill fly reel. I'd bought a Wright McGill 4/5 weight rod the week before and this was to be its mate. I'd taken the reel to work to show to a buddy of mine, who was just getting into fly fishing and looking for his first reel. It was a Friday, about noon, I called home from the job and suggested to my wife that she pack a picnic dinner and we'd go out on the boat that evening and I'd try out my new reel. You'd think that at 57, having fished since before memory, I'd be a little more sedate than that, but on this particular day, it wasn't so.

I hurried home. Friday traffic is always bad, but on this Friday, it seemed impossibly slow. I finally made it home about 5:30. My wife, Sharon, was pretty much ready to go. I still had to spool line on the reel. Something I hadn't taken into account earlier, when I'd made the call. I decided to pull a 5 weight line off an old Martin reel and, in my haste, decided to wind the line and backing on my left arm, thumb to elbow, instead of finding something to use as a spindle. I'm sure that it was at this point, though I couldn't have noticed it at the time, that there was a subtle shift in the wind. Behind a far off cloud, there was a barely audible rumble of thunder, as one of the fishing gods woke from his slumber and raised an eyebrow to better see what was happening.

One of the great attractions of fishing, unless you're a professional, competitive angler, is that it is about relaxation. It is not to be hurried or rushed. Over the years, I'd come to realize that, and to savor, like a fine wine or whiskey, all the moments involved in a fishing trip, from anticipation, through preparation and the actual trip, to the wind down and stowage of equipment. Since this realization, the fishing gods have generally smiled upon me. Things have usually gone as planned, save the few minor glitches that are necessary to keep things interesting.

Today, all such wisdom had escaped me. I had a new toy, and I wanted to play with it! I'm sure, by now, the fishing god assigned to this outing was watching carefully, sighing with exasperation, at the pace at which I was trying to perform the line transfer. When I had the Martin emptied of the 100 foot line and 70 yards of backing, I asked my wife to hold the combination, as though it were knitting yarn, while I wound it in my new reel. She was doing so when the phone rang. She carefully laid the loops down and picked up the phone. Someone wanted us to donate to some campaign. I'll bet that it was then that the fishing god cracked his first grin. Sharon picked the loops back up and we continued. Maybe it was having laid them down. Maybe I was winding the reel too fast. Maybe the forces of friction and inertia caused the first couple of loops to jump from her hands. *Maybe* there were *other* forces at work, but jump they did and "all the Kings horses…" or, our best efforts couldn't get the loops properly sequenced again. After a while, it was probably minutes, but seemed to me like hours, we gave up trying to load the reel and started picking at the rats nest that had somehow materialized where those beautiful, concentric loops had once been. By now, I'd guess that old fishing god was in a full belly laugh and probably elbowing the one next him saying "look at what I did to ole Fred." The line itself wasn't all that hard to make right, but the backing proved to be more than my old fat fingers and aging eyes could overcome. Out came the knife and I settled for about 30 yards of backing. Okay, I was ready to go ! I looked out the window and it was getting dark. If we *hurried*, we could probably get an hour in before it was too dark to see…there's that word again. I looked at Sharon and I could see that her enthusiasm had waned. The fish were safe for the night.

Chicken salad sandwiches, cut veggies, chips and an ice cold brew (a great boat supper) aren't so bad in an easy chair in front of a good movie either. Later, I stepped out onto the front porch and gazed up at the night sky. The twinkling stars seemed, a little off, as though there were a wry humor in them and a far off owl hooted with glee. Maybe it was just me.

As for the fishing gods, I guess they decided I'd been sufficiently chastised for my transgression. Sharon and I, and I suspect that other fellow, the one who laughed all night, went out the next morning and had a good day. No spectacular catches, but we eased slowly from cove to cove and around each promising point, boating a few and cherishing the time. I enjoyed every unhurried moment.

The Trout Cup

It sat there, inconspicuous, innocuous, on the knick knack shelf. It was large for a coffee mug, too small to be a beer mug. For the most part it was beige in color with a few chips and dings that showed that it had been well used. What made it unique, or at least attracted my eye, was the raised, beautifully painted, jumping, square tail brook trout that was on the face of the mug, opposite the handle. Unlike the rest of the cup, the trout showed no signs of wear. That seemed odd to me since it protruded from the surface of the cup, I would have thought that it would have taken the most abuse, but there it was bright and shiny as though it had been painted yesterday. My uncle Dell had just started a pot of coffee and we were moving from the kitchen toward the living room of his cozy mobile home just outside of Berlin, Vermont, waiting for it to brew, when the mug caught my eye. It had been a few years since I'd visited

Uncle Dell and I didn't recall seeing the mug before. I asked him where he'd come by it. "That" he said. "Oh that's my magic trout mug. I've had that for years and years, but now it's time to pass it on."

"Dell" I said "you know I'm an avid fisherman. If you don't want the mug, I'd be proud to take it!"

He folded his long lanky frame into one of the easy chairs and motioned me to do the same. Then he began telling me of a fishing trip he took, many years ago, up in Vermont's Northeast Kingdom. After fishing a few of his regular holes, with little success, he decided to follow a small unnamed stream up a mountain to see what it might produce. As best as he could recall, he was in his twenties or thirties then, which would make it ten or so years before I was born, as he was about eighty as we spoke.

"Back then I was strictly a trout fisherman, I didn't bother with perch or pike. When I went fishing it was on the streams and beaver dams up in the Kingdom" he began.

"I hiked along the stream for quite a while, not seeing any water that looked especially promising, but decided to press on" he said. "I climbed on and eventually came upon a small pool beneath a four foot fall. I knew there'd be trout in there. Question was could I catch 'em. The tree limbs were so thick that it would be tough to approach and get any kind of cast without spooking the fish so I decided to try a belly crawl up to the head of the pool. I'd then let my line just float down with the current and see what happened. So crawl I did across those damp, slippery, mossy rocks and eventually I got to where I could let my line down into the water."

The coffee was ready and Dell paused his tale while I got up and poured us each a cup.

"I eased my size fourteen Adams onto the water without even a hint of a ripple and let it drift down the length of the pool. Nothing. I stripped it back and tried it again, as carefully as the first. Nothing. I tried a third time, same result. Surely, I said to myself, there are fish in here, I must be doing something wrong. I had pretty much decided to move on. I rolled over to get up and that's when I saw it. It was wedged in a little nook formed by three rocks. Its top had been sealed with a piece wood that sat snugly in the opening. I pulled the wood out and inside was this note."

He reached into a drawer in the table beside him, pulled out a very old piece of paper and handed it to me. Dell took a sip of coffee as I read the words out loud. "If you've found this then I can rest easy that you are truly a trouter. If that be so, this mug will bring you good fortune on all your fishing expeditions. But, beware, if you are not true to the trout, if you waste your time in pursuit of other fishes, this vessel will bring upon you a curse that will allow you to catch no trout at all. So! Before you decide to take this mug with you, you must decide that you are devoted to the trout. This mug has been with me since I was a young man. I came upon it much like you have and I know that the magic of the mug is real. There are indeed trout in this pool and if you take this cup and dip a drink from the pool, they will be yours today, but you will be committed, from that point on to fishing solely for trout." The note wasn't signed.

"I was thirsty anyway" continued Dell, as I handed back the note. "so I dipped the cup into the pool and drank of its cold, clear water. Then, on a whim, I decided to float the fly down the pool one more time. It hadn't traveled five feet when there was a flash from below and a fine fish took. I brought it in and admired the beauty of the eight inch brookie. The pool was small and I figured that the fight had spooked any other fish it might hold, but I decided one more try was in order. I laid the fly on the water, and fed line out, ten feet later, another strike. This one was a little better, maybe nine, nine and a half inches. I looked at the cup and a shiver came over me. This was the very same fly and very same tactic that had produced no fish, only a few minutes before. Two trout would be enough for dinner that night, so I left the pool, cup in hand, and started back down. It was near dark when I got back to the camp site. I pulled out my tin of bacon grease, cut up a potato, and enjoyed my meal. I found my pint of rye and started to pour some into my new found mug. I hesitated for a moment, not knowing if spirits were appropriate. Then I decided it was a fisherman's mug, of course it would welcome a shot or two. I sat, cradling the cup in both hands, staring at the fire until it was only embers, wondering about the power of the mug. From that day on, I carried the mug with me when I went fishing and it seemed like I was never skunked. If I fished with a friend, I always out fished him. I never abused the power of the mug. I never kept more than a meal's worth. Why should I, I'd catch more tomorrow if I tried? Over the years, the mug took quite a beating. I must have knocked it against rocks a dozen times or more, certainly hard enough to break the normal ceramic coffee mug. Though it chipped a mite here and there, it never broke, never cracked. For years and years, I remained true to the mug. Then as I got older and the knees and ankles started complaining more and more loudly about slippery rocks, ice cold water, and steep mountainsides. I decided to fish from boats. Lakes, even trout ponds, hold other fish and I remember the feeling in my gut when I landed that first little small mouth bass. I knew my trout fishing days were over. Oh I tried for a while, but I knew deep inside that my efforts were for naught. After a while I quit carrying the cup with me. It seemed almost a sacrilege to have it on me while I fished for perch, or bass, or pike. I put it in the cupboard for a long time but, about a month ago I got the urge to take it out. I thought about passing it along to somebody I know, but I don't know anyone who fishes solely for trout. Besides, it may be as much a curse as a blessing. I don't think these old legs will take me back where I found it. I've written my note of admonishment to the next owner. I just don't know where to leave it."

I was jealous. I coveted that mug. Truth was, I didn't qualify to own it and never would. I've been pursuing warm water fish for as long as I can remember, and though I fish for trout, I could never do so exclusively. So I held it one more time, admiring the trout a little longer, thanked Dell for the entertaining story and bid him good night.

Dell was ninety when he passed away. Sometime between the time he told me the story and then, he must have decided what to do, for the mug was not to be found. He may have hidden it in the rocks beside some obscure stream. It may be on some table at a flea market. Now that we are in the computer age, you may, some day, see it on e-bay. It may have mysteriously found its way back to the spot where Dell found it. Should you chance upon it, no matter where, if you are a trout man, claim it for your own. You will have great success and gain admiration from your peers. But, if you do, realize that you are thenceforth and forevermore committed to the pursuit of trout. Be not tempted to fish for other species unless you a willing to forego the one you love most.

Evolution

I sat here for the longest time, trying to remember the first time I went fishing. I couldn't do it. I tried and tried, I gritted my teeth, I squinted my eyes. I just couldn't do it. But I did remember the first time I remember going fishing and that'll have to do. So that's what I'm asking you to recall right now. Lean back, take a deep breath, close your eyes, and conjure up that day. I'll still be here when you get back. Welcome back! Great day wasn't it? I'll bet you were all excited about going fishing. Your very first remembered moment of the sport had nothing to do with catching fish, it was all about the act of going fishing. I don't know who took you, maybe your dad, an uncle, brother, or mother or sister. I do know it was someone who loved you. It is an act of love to initiate a child to the sport/art of fishing, knowing the difficulties that one is about to encounter, while the young one gradually learns the myriad things a fisherman needs to know. What I really wanted you to recall, though, is that your excitement, your enthusiasm was for the act, not the results. It stays that way for a long time. I remember the thrill of going out at night, after a rainy day, flashlight in hand collecting night crawlers for the next day's fishing. It was fun. It wasn't a chore. Digging worms was fun. Biking with a buddy to the nearest body of water and fishing for hours for little perch or sunnies was fun. As a matter of fact, it was more than fun, it was a great way, maybe the best way, to spend a summer day. I don't know if it happens to all of us, most of us, or just some of us. Hell maybe it only happened to me but, somewhere along the line, my focus, my purpose somehow transmuted to the size and numbers of fish that I could land. Success became measured in numbers and pounds. It's understandable. As skills increase, so do expectations. Over the years, tackle gets upgraded. Wood or steel gives way to fiberglass and that, in turn, to graphite. The wooden rowboat becomes a fiberglass water rocket pushed by as much horsepower as an automobile so that one can get to "where they are" at highway speed. And, on it are probably some kind of electronic devices, like a fish finder and, or GPS to help locate the finny creatures that, once, when we were young, before we became scientific, we could simply outsmart. In all this gain, something's lost. The simple act of fishing becomes a project. Blissful simplicity is sacrificed to technology, so that more fish can be boated. And, while the sport is still great, it isn't quite the same innocent joy it once was.

Then, for some of us (at least for me) something happens, an inexplicable metamorphosis, there comes a moment of realization, a nearly supernatural sense that we've lost the true purpose of fishing, the secret magic that made us fall in love with the pastime in the first place. We decide to "simplify" the process. Oh we already have all the expensive tackle, so we might as well continue to use it, but our "favorite" rod becomes one that we've had for years, or maybe one that reminds us of bygone days. Maybe we decide to turn off the fish finder and try drifting to find structure, or triangulating a productive spot. We used to do it that way. Maybe we sight-fish structure letting our fishing sense, our experience, our inner voices tell us where the fish should be. Many, like myself, decide to fly-fish, almost exclusively. It is a great, but decidedly less efficient method of procuring denizens from the deep. Why would we do this? Why make it harder on ourselves? It's our way of remembering that fishing does not require catching to be enjoyed. And the reward, when it comes, is ever so slightly sweeter for having "done it the hard way'. And, strangely, subtly, it seems as if nature, Mother Nature if you will, realizes the transformation that has taken place within us and smiles upon us and rewards us with subconscious, almost Zen like moments of awe and wonder while we fish, and, on more occasions than we rightly deserve, she sees fit to hand up some beautiful specimens from the water.

Experience

When you've been at this fishing thing for over fifty years, as I have, you get lulled into a sense of "know it all", a "been there, done that, seen it all before" attitude. Well I'm here to tell you that, as the old song says, "it ain't necessarily so". Now don't get me wrong, I may, in time, resume that way of thinking, but for now I'm of the mind that no matter what I've seen or done, the fishing gods can still throw me a curve.

I can recall fishing an old abandoned quarry at night with my buddy, Vern. Vern was using a Jitterbug. All of sudden, I hear him let out a whoop. Now Vern's been around for a while and I figure it must be something special to get him all excited so I run over to where he's fishing. As I get close enough to see what's going on, I notice the most peculiar thing. The line leaving Vern's rod is going up not down into the water. Well eventually the mystery came to light when the Great Horned

Owl rose above the side of the quarry and we could see it. It had swooped down on what it thought was a frog and had imbedded one point of one of the treble hooks in its talon. It took Vern forever to bring the owl in and then another forever for the two of us to extricate the lure from the talon without getting punctured ourselves. The fishing gods had deemed that we were not to catch fish that night.

Most fishermen have a snake story or two. Like the time my friend Charlie and I were canoeing the Shenandoah and a snake fell out of a tree and into the canoe. We managed to get the creature out of the canoe, but it shook us so that we spent the rest of the float looking into trees rather than for likely spots to cast to. Again, it was not a productive day.

Then there was the time I was wade fishing for smallmouth bass in the Rappahannock River at Kelly's Ford. (Incidentally this stretch is post card or calendar cover beautiful and easy to get to from Northern Virginia.) Anyway, I stepped off a rock into a deep hole. By the time I bobbed back up, the current had carried me downstream a considerable distance. When I did break surface, I was maybe fifteen feet away from a beaver that was swimming upstream. At that distance, its eyes were huge and its incisors enormous. It was evidently as frightened as I and it quickly turned and swam away, but it took me some time to get my heart down out of my throat and my mind back to casting for fish.

I could go on forever about sudden squalls and rapids and floating into electric fences, but you get my drift. After a while you pretty much think there ain't no more, but last summer I was proven wrong.

On this particular day, late May as I recall, my son, son in law and I were fishing the small lake where I live from my pontoon boat, a decidedly less adventurous type of fishing than wading or floating rivers and less likely to precipitate an unusual adventure. We'd been out since just after dawn and had made our way to the dam at the east end of the lake. We had made one pass along the length of the dam, casting into the large rocks that form the out layer of the dam itself. We had eased along on the trolling motor and had reached the north end where the dam meets the shore. There had been some discussion about making another pass at the dam, but we had decided to fish east along the north shore for a while. So there we were, Jim, my son, throwing some kind of soft plastic and Randy and I each casting a fly. All three of us intent on the shore line we were working when there was a tremendous thud. I remember muttering "what the" as I spun around, annoyed that someone was disturbing our fishing.

My annoyance turned to a moment of panic as what I saw was a single engine airplane planing across the water in our direction. It hadn't skated far when it came to rest, relieving my fear that it was going to ram us. I remember thinking that the lake really wasn't large enough for a sea plane and that it'd probably have trouble getting air borne again. Then I realized that the plane had no pontoons. It hadn't landed, but rather crash landed onto the lake. I told my companions to reel in, that we were going over to the plane. I don't think they had quite reached the same conclusion as I had as there were some comments about another cast, or he'll be alright, but I insisted. In my haste, I managed to hook my fly in one of the bow fender lines so by the time we reached the plane, I had about half a spool of fly line trailing along in the water. By the time we got to the plane, it was over half submerged with only the tail sticking up in the air. The pilot was unharmed and had escaped the plane. We got him aboard the boat and watched the plane slip into the depths of the lake. My depth finder indicated that we were in about ninety feet of water. The pilot, wet and cold, recounted how the plane's engine had just quit and he had been forced to glide into the lake rather than crash into the community that surrounds it; which explained why we hadn't heard anything until the impact. By the time he had finished his tale, I'd managed to get my line back on the reel and extricate the hook from the fender line. Randy, my son in law, had his cell phone with him and let the pilot call home. They, in turn, called the authorities and soon the dam was awash with a visual cacophony of red, blue, and amber lights flashing from the tops of the police, fire and rescue vehicles strung along the its entire top. The police asked us to hang around so they could take our statements. Then we were told that the Fire Marshall was on his way and wanted to take statements from us so we had to wait for his arrival. All in all it cost us about three hours of fishing, except for Randy who stood in the boat doggedly defying the fishing deities that had schemed to cut short our outing, casting his five weight along the dam shore, in about eight inches of water. Our day was scuttled, but not nearly as bad as the pilot's

Come to think of it, when the fishing gods are reduced to throwing airplanes out of the sky to quash your trip, maybe, just maybe, you have pretty much seen it all and if not, what could be next?

In Quest of Trout
(A Fishing Lesson)

SEEKING TROUT, I HIKED ONE DAY
TO A SHADED STREAM WHERE THE RAINBOWS PLAY

BUT AS I REACHED MY SECRET SPOT
KNOWN BUT TO ME OR SO I THOUGHT

I STOOD AGHAST AND IN DESPAIR
FOR AN OLD MAN LAY NAPPING THERE

HIS HEAD WAS PROPPED AGAINST A TREE
HIS BAMBOO ROD LAY 'CROSS HIS KNEE

"OLD MAN" I SAID AND LOUDLY SPOKE
HE YAWNED AND STRECHED AS HE AWOKE

AND AS OUR FISHER'S WILLS COLLIDED
"YOU WASTE THIS PLACE" I SOUNDLY CHIDED

HE RAISED ONE EYE AND LOOKING SMUG
REACHED 'ROUND THE TREE, BROUGHT FORTH A
JUG

HIS EYES HE SHADED FROM THE SUN
HE TURNED IT UP BUT OFFERED NONE

"I KNOW A PLACE" THE OLD MAN SPOKE
HE DIDN'T SMILE HE DIDN'T CHOKE

WHERE RAINBOW TROUT ARE THICK AS FLIES
AND YOU NEED BOTH ARMS TO SHOW THEIR SIZE

"OLD MAN YOU'RE DAFT" I SHOWED MY SCORN
"YOU'VE PULLED TOO MUCH UPON YOUR CORN"

"YOUNG MAN" HE SAID "I KNOW NOT WHY
YOU ABUSE ME SO, I'VE TOLD NO LIE

THE JOURNEY THERE IT ISN'T LONG
AND ALL THE WHILE THE STREAM SINGS SONG

IT TAKES A SOUL FROM WOE AND CARE
THE SIMPLE ACT OF GOING THERE

I WAS THERE WHEN YOU CAME TODAY
AND I'LL RETURN WHEN YOU GO AWAY"

The Wiley 'Bow

Is that a caddis fly I see
Oh I guess it just might be
Or an angler tempting me
I'll swim by to closer see
I'll swim close and careful look
For once a caddis fly I took
From a pool just up the brook
Unaware it had a hook
I felt the sting of cold steel raw
And there was pain within my jaw
But I shook free just as I saw
Man reach out his loathsome paw
Near the riffle I'll swim and play
And from this caddis shy away
I think I'll wait another day
For a caddis fly to float my way

Insanity

It's a psychotic predilection
A malevolent affliction
Insanity he'll not deny
That spurs a man to venture forth
With a ball of fuzz and piece of steel
He's somehow dubbed a fly

As the sane all raise an eye

On cold gray morn
Or dead of night
Or when the sun is high
With a wooden stick
And a strand of silk
He'll wander low and high
With a ball of fuzz and piece of steel
He's somehow dubbed a fly

And the sane just let him by

He'll wade a stream
T'would turn to ice

If somehow it were stilled
'Till his very marrow
Pains him it's so chilled
With a ball of fuzz and piece of steel
He's somehow dubbed a fly

And the sane will wonder why

He's off chasing rainbows
In waters yon and nigh
With a ball of fuzz and piece of steel
He's somehow dubbed a fly
And, a rainbow won
He'll set it free with a gentle sigh

And the sane will want to cry

But they'll laugh at him
And slap their thigh
At his wooden stick, strand of silk,
Ball of fuzz and piece of steel
He's somehow dubbed a fly

And though the sane may try

They'll never ken
His heart within
The gleam upon his eye
As he ventures forth
With a ball of fuzz and piece of steel
He's somehow dubbed a fly.

The Cast

T'was no monster fish as I recall
In fact it was rather small
But had I made a lesser cast
T'would have been no fish at all

Ron

THREE OR FOUR DAYS
MOST EVERY YEAR
FOR MANY YEARS BYGONE
I TRAVELED NORTH AND FISHED CHAMPLAIN
WITH MY COUSIN, RON
WE SOAKED BAIT
FOR YELLOW PERCH
AND TROLLED FOR NORTHERN PIKE
AND CAST OUR LURES
TOWARD ROCKY SHORES
FOR SMALLMOUTH AND THE LIKE
SOMETIMES WE TALKED OF POLITICS
SOMETIMES FOOTBALL FILLED THE AIR
SOMETIMES WE SHARED A SILENCE
ONLY FISHERMEN CAN SHARE
WE FISHED AT DUSK
WE FISHED AT DAWN
AND THE HOURS THEY WERE SPECIAL
THOSE SPENT WITH COUSIN RON

MY WIFE, SHARON AND MY AUNT BERN
WOULD BE WAITNG AT THE CAMP

AND WE'D RETURN IN TIME TO EAT
COLD AND SOMETIMES DAMP
THE CARDS 'D BE ON THE TABLE
AS WOULD THE CRIBBAGE BOARD
WE FOUR WOULD PLAY
AND LAUGH AND DRINK
IN KINSHIP AND ACCORD
YOU COULD HEAR OUR SHOUTS OF "FIFTEEN TWO"
NEAR THE WHOLE NIGHT LONG
AND THE MASTER AT THAT TABLE
WAS MY COUSIN, RON

RON NOW FISHES THAT COLD DEEP WATER
I CALL "LAKE BEYOND THE CLOUDS"
WHERE HE'S NO LONGER BOTHERED
BY JET SKIS, JOB, OR CROWDS
AND I'M SURE THAT AS HE PLIES THAT LAKE
HE'LL BE MARKING SPOTS FOR ME
FOR COUSIN RON WAS THE FISHING BUDDY
ANY ANGLER WOULD WISH TO BE
I DOUBT THAT I'LL E'RE WET A LINE
BUT WHAT I'LL THINK OF HIM
THE SPARKLE IN HIS EYE
THE HUMOR IN HIS GRIN

FOR QUITE SOME YEARS
I'VE OWNED A NO NAME BOAT
NO NAME APPEALED TO ME
BUT WHEN IT HITS THE WATER NEXT
IT'LL BE THE *RONALD B.*

Printed in the United States
215972BV00001B/99/P

9 781608 138869